# UNEARTHED

Gina Ranallli

## Also by Gina Ranalli

*Dark Surge*

*Rumors of My Death*

*Chemical Gardens*

*Mother Puncher*

*Wall of Kiss*

*Suicide Girls in the Afterlife*

*Sky Tongues*

*House of Fallen Trees*

*Praise the Dead*

*Ghost Chant*

# UNEARTHED

# CHAPTER 1

The rain had fallen hard for six straight days and the muddy ground sucked at Rebecca Robinson's boots as she approached the edge of her property calling for her dog.

The sky churned shades of gray that wrestled and rolled against each other like lovers, or maybe enemies.

"Lou!" she yelled, nearing the tree line that marked the beginning of 900 acres of wild forest. *Where has that dog gotten off to?*

She stopped, frowning into the woods, listening for the sound of paws tramping through underbrush or distant teasing barks, but there was nothing.

No birdsong, no insect drone, not even the rustle of branches scraping back and forth against one another.

Glancing back up at the sky to ensure that she had indeed seen evidence of wind, a feeling of uneasiness began to creep around in her belly. Boiling clouds spun across the heavens, chased by others as far as the eye could see.

And yet, nothing moved on the ground. No leaves

tumbled by, not a single blade of grass stirred, Rebecca's long dark hair lay flat against her back, completely undisturbed.

Worried, she peered into the darkness of the forest, hoping for some glimpse of movement, a flash of white fur. "Lou?" she called again, hearing the nervousness in her voice. "Come on, boy. Time to eat."

Above, the sky broke open again and she became immediately drenched to the skin. Cussing, she turned back to the house, hoping the dog might be back on the porch, having approached from a different direction, and sure enough, there he was, dripping wet, panting happily while eyeing her with what appeared to be amusement.

Cursing still, she started back to the house, thinking about starting a fire and boiling water for tea before peeling the soaked clothing from her skin. She kept her eyes on the ground, her boots sinking nearly ankle-deep into the muck that was her land. The land, the house and the dog were all she had to show for twenty years of marriage and one year of widowhood. The cancer that had taken her husband Glen at forty-two had torn her heart from her chest but had been unable to touch the more substantial objects of her world.

Fifty feet away, Lou barked suddenly, causing her to look up just as the ground beneath her feet gave way. Crying out, she leapt backwards as the ground collapsed in on itself, creating a sinkhole the size of a child's swimming pool.

Recovering her balance, she back-peddled until the ground felt solid enough to stand on. From the porch, Lou continued to bark. Rainwater ran off the end of her nose as she cautiously approached the ragged edge of the hole, trying to see just how deep it went.

Small stones and mud slid down the sides of the 4x4

hole, slipping away into what appeared to be a bottomless pit. Squinting against the rain, she stepped closer to the edge and gasped when the ground gave way once more. Rebecca fell into a sitting position on the edge of the sinkhole, legs dangling down into the darkness, hands seeking purchase and coming back with fistfuls of mud. The earth under my her disappeared and she scrambled backwards like a desperate crab, the ground vanishing the moment her weight touched it.

*Hollow*, she thought frantically. *The earth is hollow and hungry and it means to swallow me alive.*

Screaming was pointless. There was no one within miles to hear, but she found herself doing it just the same. Lou's barking turned panicked and she was dimly aware of his presence, closer now, just on the other side of the ever-growing hole, and then the ground was solid again, firm enough to hold her weight as she leapt to her feet and skittered back towards the tree line. Only when she had reached the lip of the forest did she feel safe enough to stop. The house seemed miles away now and between her and it was a sinkhole large enough to swallow a car.

"Jesus Christ," she panted, bent at the waist, hands on knees. Rain continued to pelt her and her hair stuck to her face in thin, tangled strands. The dog raced to her side and jumped up, leaving muddy paw prints on her thighs. Absently, she rubbed his wet head before nudging him away.

Straightening up, she saw just how filthy she was and groaned inwardly. Lou continued to yap at her as she turned her attention back to the sinkhole and shivered. To the best of her knowledge it was the first time the earth had opened up anywhere on her property and she couldn't help but wonder just how much of the land was hollow. The thought made her queasy; if the land was unfit to build on, selling it would difficult, if not impossible, unless she was prepared to take a pittance.

She sighed at the prospect of having to get an appraiser to come out, but decided she'd wait until after the rainy season had ended. Maybe it wouldn't be so bad.

Glancing down at Lou, she said, "What do you say we get out of this rain, huh, boy?"

The dog wagged his bushy tail, happy despite looking like he'd been trudging up and down a muddy river. Rebecca imagined she looked even worse as they started back to the house, giving the sinkhole a wide berth.

There was a moment when the dog paused to stare at the hole, a low growl rumbling up from deep within his chest, but Rebecca called him on and he followed without hesitation.

Back inside, she toweled Lou off before running herself a steaming bath and scrubbing the mud and grime from her skin. Once clean, she felt a little better—less shaky from the close call with the sinkhole-and with every passing moment could see the absurdity in what had been sheer panic. Obviously, even if she'd fallen into the hole, it wouldn't have been tragic. It's not like she would have disappeared into the center of the Earth. Probably no more than six or seven feet at most and plenty easy enough to climb out. True, she would have emerged looking like some kind of mud monster, but she'd come pretty close to that anyway.

Sitting in her favorite recliner with a hot cup of tea, she chuckled at her own silliness. Just a middle-aged woman out in the boonies, scared of taking a little spill.

Shaking her head, she reached for the TV remote and pressed the power button, only to be greeted with white noise on every station. She turned it off again, frustrated but not particularly surprised. There was no cable out here and losing power was far from an unusual occurrence.

Lou looked up at Rebecca from his spot on an old braided rug by the fireplace, his brown eyes questioning.

"You look like you could use a bath too," she told him. "Would have been nice if I'd thought to do it before you ran all over the house and—"

A tremendous crashing sound cut her off and caused the dog to leap to his feet, barking hysterically. The house shook; a framed photograph of her deceased husband, smiling in the long ago sunshine, tumbled from the mantle and shattered on the stone hearth.

Flinching, Rebecca's first thought was that a bomb had exploded somewhere nearby, but a moment later she recognized the sound, though she'd never heard it amplified by what had to be times ten.

A falling tree.

But, no. Not this time. Not just one tree, but many, judging by the way the earth trembled beneath the force of God only knew how many tons of 100 foot pines. It had felt as though the house had been grasped by a great hand, lifted and then dropped again.

"What the...?"

Moving to the front bay window, she stared out at the tree line, searching for-she didn't know what. A wave of falling trees? She shook her head, feeling ridiculous, and turned back to the dog.

"One tree knocked down another," she muttered. "Nothing unusual about that."

Lou barked again, evidently disagreeing with her.

"Dumb dog."

Her eyes fell to the unopened bottle of champagne still on the mantle, the first real reminder she'd had all morning that today was New Year's Day. Suddenly she forgot all about the rain, the dog, the sinkhole and the falling trees.

She went to the old, over-stuffed sofa and sank down into it, part of her wishing she'd drank the bottle the night before, as she'd planned.

*If I had, I wouldn't be feeling this hollow ache right now, remembering that Glen had proposed to me on that snowy New Year's Eve so many years before.*

She had wanted to toast her dead husband, had bought the bottle for that very occasion, a desire to remember.

But in the end, she hadn't been able to go through with it. She'd been a coward, afraid the memories would be painful instead of joyful.

Just a stupid, frightened woman, still scared of phantoms in places where there should have been only love.

Lou whined, nudging Rebecca's hand with his muzzle.

She blinked. "Another year without Daddy," she told the dog absently. "Can you believe it?"

Lou's brown eyes watched her quizzically, his ears still twitching slightly at the word *daddy* and Rebecca felt her heart break all over again.

*I should have just gotten shitfaced and slept through the day.*

Another thud shook the house and both she and the dog cried out in alarm. Whatever it was, it sounded closer this time and Rebecca leapt to her feet.

"Jesus! What *is* that?"

Her closest neighbors, the Days, sometimes had better TV reception and she decided to give them a call. Crossing the house into the kitchen, Lou padded beside her, his tail tucked down between his legs. As she dialed, the dog growled softly, his eyes fixed on the back door.

"Shh," she told him. "It's okay."

On the other end of the line, the Days phone rang six

times and then an answering service clicked on. She waited through the out-going message and then said, "Hey, guys, it's Rebecca. I guess you may have gone away for the holiday, but if you get this, can you give me a call? I keep hearing these loud thuds and I'm just wondering what's going on. Now that I'm saying this out loud, it sounds pretty ridiculous." She felt herself blushing, but soldiered on. "Anyway, I doubt it's any kind of construction happening since its New Year's morning, but, I don't know. Give me a buzz, okay? Bye."

She hung up, feeling like a complete fool. Looking down at Lou, she said, "Well, they'll probably think I'm nuts now, huh?"

Then again, most people thought she was a tad peculiar these days, living out here by herself, with little to no contact with the rest of the world. No real friends to speak of, unless you counted the four-legged variety. But she'd learned the hard way-being close to people got you one thing, every time, without fail: hurt.

She was having none of that anymore.

Opening her mouth to say as much to the dog, she froze, wondering what that new sound was.

The clock above the stove ticked in time with her heart. She could hear nothing else.

The new sound was no sound at all.

The rain had stopped.

A beam of sunlight abruptly shot through the windows, blinding in its brightness. The clouds were parting and she smiled despite her bewilderment

"Happy New Year," she said and the entire house lurched to one side, throwing her to the floor as cupboards opened and dishes, mugs and glasses flew out, shattering all around her. Rebecca lifted one arm to shield her face while instinctively attempting to cover the dog's body with her own.

Things crashed in other parts of the house; furniture slid across floors and slammed into walls.

She bit back a scream, squeezed her eyes closed and waited for the world to stop careening.

And then it did.

They were left with the sound of tinkling glass and an occasional bang-maybe from a book falling from a shelf-but the house had gone still once more.

Opening her eyes, she saw that her house had pitched sideways and now rested at a 40 degree angle. Getting back to the living room would mean walking up a steep incline.

Lou whimpered beside her and she knew she had to get the dog out of there. Broken glass covered virtually every inch of the floor-there was no way she could let him walk around in it.

She knew what had happened now. It was another sinkhole. Had to be. There was no other explanation.

Struggling to her feet, she lifted the terrified dog in her arms and, glass crunching underfoot, made her way to the back door and into the sudden strange light of the New Year.

# CHAPTER 2

Three miles North, inside the Pinecone Cafe, Joe Morris had just finished prepping the grill when the world shook and almost caused him to lose his footing.

"Holy shit!"

He turned and looked over the counter at Stacy who sat bleary-eyed, smoking a Pall Mall despite being three months pregnant. "What the hell was that?" she asked.

He shrugged. "Earthquake, I guess. Big one too."

The frying pans hanging over the grill swung, clanking together loudly.

"Since when do we have big earthquakes?" Stacy asked.

"It's been known to happen. Remember the one that hit Olympia a few years back?"

"That was nothing," she said, mashing out her cigarette. "Not compared to the ones they get in other countries. Or even in California."

Joe didn't reply, his ear cocked. From the used car lot next door, an alarm was sounding. "Fuck," he muttered. "If that's not one of the cars, who knows how long we'll have to listen to it."

"It's one of the cars," Stacy said. "Probably that yellow Ram. I think it's the only one over there worth more than a couple grand."

The used car lot was a bit of a joke to the locals. It went in and out of business every few months, always being bought by new owners and most people suspected it was a cover for drug dealers who were too stupid to realize there wasn't much money to be made that way around here. Eventually, they learned and packed up and moved on, probably to the city.

Joe didn't know if the drug dealer story was true or not. He just wished whoever bought the place last would stay in business for a while. Potential customers for them meant potential customers for him.

He reached up to steady the swinging pans, glancing around the kitchen area to be sure nothing had fallen to the floor.

"I can't believe we're even open today," Stacy said, already uninterested in the earthquake. "Who the hell comes to a greasy spoon on New Year's Day?"

"People still gotta eat, Stace," Joe said.

"No doubt, but most of them will be either hung over and the thought of eating your eggs and bacon will make them puke or they're having breakfast with their families, which is what we should be doing."

Looking over his shoulder at her, Joe smiled. "You know you're my only family."

Stacy snorted. "Likewise. And how sad is that?"

"Pretty sad," he agreed.

And it was too. At forty-five, Joe had been divorced for over seven years, never saw his three sons who'd moved out of state with their mom, and had lived alone ever since.

Stacy was in her mid-twenties and pregnant by some guy she'd met in a bar one night and never saw again. Her story was even more sad than Joe's: family, including one sister, had been killed in a car wreck when she was fourteen and she'd pretty much been on her own ever since.

They were both loners, thrown together by circumstance-Joe owned the Pinecone Cafe and Stacy waitressed there full-time. He also employed a couple part-timers but they both had real lives and were spending the holiday elsewhere.

"Think we'll actually get any customers today?" Stacy asked.

"Don't know. Remember last year we got a few around noon and..."

The small building shook again. Light fixtures swung and salt and pepper shakers rattled against table tops. When it was over, Joe tried to hide his frazzled nerves and chuckled. "Aftershock, probably."

Giving his a skeptical look, Stacy slid off the barstool and walked across the diner to peer out the window at the parking lot. "At least the rain stopped," she said.

From her vantage point, she could see past their own lot to the one next door, which housed about two dozen storage units. Across the street was The Motorcycle Barn, where the local bikers tended to gather most weeknights when they ran out of drinking money.

"I bet you could hear a pin drop out there," she said. "I haven't seen a single car drive by."

Turning back to the grill, Joe said, "Well, like you said, it's New Year's morning. Probably most folks ain't even awake yet." He paused, then asked, "You fill up those napkin dispensers yet?"

Facing him once more, Stacy said, "Was just gonna get

to it after I finished my smoke."

"Well, you're finished. Hop to it, Missy."

Stacy gave Joe's back the finger, which he evidently knew she would because without bothering to glance at her, he said, "And fuck you too, Sunshine."

A couple minutes later, Stacy emerged from the storage room carrying several stacks of bound paper napkins and Joe used the remote control to turn on the television suspended in a far corner of the dining area. He groaned when he could find nothing but static on any channel.

"Maybe the cable's out," Stacy offered without looking up from her task.

"You think so, Einstein?"

"Hey, don't get bitchy with me, old man. You probably forgot to pay the bill with your Alzheimer's setting in and all."

"Cute."

The bell over the entrance door clanged and they both looked up to see a disheveled man stagger into the diner, drying blood caked in his hairline and trickling down his forehead. His clothes and hands were covered in mud and his eyes tore around the diner frantically.

"I need a phone," the stranger gasped, stumbling forward towards where Stacy sat in one of the booths, a napkin dispenser open before her.

"Whoa, whoa, whoa." Joe quickly moved out of the kitchen and approached the man, holding out a hand. "You okay, partner? You wreck your car or something?"

The man regarded Joe briefly as if he were an alien, then he blurted out laughter. "Wreck my car?" he brayed. "My fucking car is gone, man. *Gone*. Swallowed by the fucking devil himself." He laughed again, lost his balance and probably would have toppled over if Joe hadn't reached out to steady him.

"He tried to eat me too," the man continued. "But I got out. Fucking-A, I did. Fuck that shit. I'm not being swallowed alive."

Joe and Stacy exchanged a glance before Joe said to the man, "Been out partying all night, huh? Well, why don't you just sit down right here and I'll get you a cup of coffee. Just brewed it and it's good and hot. Fix you right up."

Turning back to Stacy, he said, "Maybe you should get the sheriff on the phone, Stace. Hopefully this guy didn't plow into anyone else when-"

The stranger pulled himself out of Joe's grasp. "I didn't wreck my car and I wasn't out partying! I'm not drunk!"

Folding his arms across his chest, Joe said, "With all due respect, sir, you just told us the devil swallowed your car. No, maybe you're not drunk, but either you're on something or you're a basket case." He looked at Stacy, eyebrows raised. She got to her feet and started towards the kitchen area where the phone was.

"The *ground* opened up, man," the muddied stranger insisted. "I was barely able to climb out of there! There's a hole in the road big enough to swallow a fucking house! Didn't you hear it?"

Joe frowned, glancing at the static on the television.

"I need to use your phone," the man repeated. "Please! I have to call my wife!"

"Phone's dead," Stacy announced, coming back around the counter. "Weird, right?"

The crease between Joe's brows deepened. "You have your cell phone on ya?"

Stacy shook her head. "It's in my coat."

"Try that."

She huffed. "Joe, you think I have the sheriff's number

on speed dial, for Christ's sake?"

"We have a phone book in the kitchen somewhere. Look it up!"

Clearly annoyed, Stacy went to do what she was told while Joe continued to study the muddy, bleeding man.

"I need to call my wife," the stranger repeated.

"You heard her," Joe said. "The phone's dead. Don't you have a cell of your own?"

"It went down with my car, man! What the fuck is wrong with you? Why aren't you listening to me?"

"Settle down," Joe told him, his patience waning. "Why don't you just have a seat and I'll get you that coffee, okay? And maybe a Band-Aid for your head."

The man reached up to touch his forehead and looked surprised when his fingers came away bloody.

"What's your name, partner?" Joe asked.

"John," he said, dejectedly as he slumped into the nearest booth. "John Ashland."

"Nice to meet you, John. I'm Joe and that spitfire over there is Stacy."

As if on cue, Stacy leaned over the counter from the kitchen and said, "Sheriff's line is busy."

"What the Christ?" Joe nearly shouted, throwing his hands up in frustration. "What? Is it the goddamn end of the world or what?"

Unintimidated by his outburst, Stacy shrugged. "It's New Year's Day, Joe. People have stuff to do."

"Look at the damn TV," he barked, gesturing towards it. "What's up with that?"

"I told you," Stacy said. "The cable's probably out."

"Bullshit." Joe walked to the door and looked out. "It's not even windy. The sky is blue."

"Maybe it got knocked out last night," Stacy said. "Christ, what's the big deal?"

But, the truth was that Joe couldn't really put into words what the big deal was. It was just a nagging sense of unease growing in the pit of his belly. Everything going out of whack at the same time and this John guy showing up, dirty and bleeding and talking nonsense.

Joe turned to face the others again. To John, he asked, "Where did you say your car got...uh...swallowed?"

"I didn't," John replied, holding a napkin to his head wound. "But not far from here. Less than a mile, probably."

Pointing outside, Joe said, "On this road? Right on 99?"

"Yeah. Why?"

"A hole big enough to swallow a house, you said." He looked at Stacy. "Could have knocked out power lines. Phone lines too, probably."

Stacy didn't reply. Instead, she went back to sitting at the counter and lit up another smoke.

"Was anyone else on the road with you when the ground caved in?" Joe asked John.

"I don't know. I don't think so. It was pretty dead out there."

"And what about when you were walking here? Did you see anyone?"

"Dude, I was running like the fucking wind. I wasn't checking out the scenery. The only reason I came in here was because I saw cars in your parking lot and figured you might be open."

Something thudded into the plate-glass window and the three of them jumped, looking up to see a creature clinging to the glass.

"Fuck!" John shouted, leaping to his feet and back-pedaling away from the front of the diner.

Joe briefly lost the ability to breathe.

The thing outside was clearly an insect-some kind of bee perhaps, but with the hard, black shell of a beetle, but that wasn't the most alarming thing about it.

What really scared the occupants of the Pinecone Cafe was that the creature was roughly the size of a coffee-table.

# CHAPTER 3

Moving across the property was precarious at best, but Rebecca was able to set Lou down and together they stood staring at what had been their home.

The house was destroyed, the east side sunk into the ground up to the bottom of the first floor windows. Looking at it from out here, Rebecca was amazed neither she nor the dog had been injured.

In truth, she was amazed they were even alive.

Just standing nearby made her nervous so she walked to the gravel driveway where her Jeep Cherokee still sat, untouched, at least for the moment.

She didn't trust that it would remain above ground for much longer though.

"Lou! Come!"

They had to get out of here, find solid ground and then worry about what came next. Was her house insured for such a catastrophe? She had no idea.

In the vehicle, she found the spare key in the visor where it had been since Glen had been alive and started the engine.

She drove, oddly calm, the dog in the passenger seat beside her, realizing that she was most likely in shock, heading for the Dailies home a mile down the road.

They'd only traveled half that distance when she had to hit the brakes, reaching an arm out to steady Lou and keep him from bashing into the dashboard.

A gaping, muddy hole yawned in the middle of the road. Easily big enough to swallow the Jeep and probably a tanker truck as well.

"*Jesus.*"

She thought there was enough space on the other side of the road and she may have been able to drive around the sinkhole, but she didn't want to take the chance. If the ground was unsteady...

Just being this close to it made her nervous.

She briefly debated trying to turn around, but there was nowhere to go. Just miles of uninhabited forest lay behind her and for the first time in her adult life, she questioned the wisdom of living out here, so far from civilization.

"Looks like we're walking, boy."

She killed the engine and got out, Lou jumping out behind her.

Together, they approached the sinkhole cautiously, taking care to not get too close, and stopping about five yards short.

Black nose twitching, Lou tried to get closer, but didn't argue when Rebecca slapped her hip and commanded, "Side!" Obediently, the dog pressed his flank against her leg and ventured no further.

She surveyed the ragged lip of the hole, trying to determine how soft the ground surrounding it might be. Several seconds passed before she realized she would just have to brave it.

Though she didn't trust driving around the hole, she knew they had no choice but to walk by it, albeit giving the monster maw a wide berth.

"Come on, Lou," she said, leading the way.

Despite managing to be several feet from the hole, the weight of their passing still caused mini-mudslides within it and Rebecca hurried by as fast as she could, releasing her pent up breath when they'd finally moved around it.

The sound of distant rumbles caused her to flinch and grit her teeth, while the dog paused to bark.

"Shh!" she scolded. She had the irrational fear that Lou's barking would cause the ground to open up further, the way a sudden loud noise could supposedly cause an avalanche. "Quiet, Lou!"

It wasn't until they had left the sinkhole about twenty yards behind them that she felt herself relax a bit. The road ahead was free of any others, at least as far as she could see.

The world around them was strangely silent. No creatures stirred in the forest flanking either side of the road. Not even birds could be heard, despite the reappearance of the sun.

Occasionally, Lou would try to run ahead, as was his usual custom when they went for walks, but each time Rebecca called him back. Not only did she fear for his safety, but she had to admit that having him near was a comfort.

This had been the case since Glen's death. She'd even taken to allowing the dog to sleep in the same bed as herself, his warm body pressed against hers, soothing her loneliness and allowing her to fall asleep to his soft dog snores. Sometimes she even thought that Lou took an equal amount of comfort from her as well.

Silly notions from the broken heart of a wounded

woman, of course, but she supposed that if they helped her get through another night, then what was the harm?

An odd droning sound startled Rebecca from her thoughts and, frowning, she turned back to face the way they'd come.

What she saw caused her jaw to drop and a tiny gasp of wonder escaped her throat.

Beside her, Lou had also turned and immediately began barking at the two huge things buzzing through the air towards them.

It was Lou's reaction that helped Rebecca realize that she should be more afraid than fascinated.

"Oh my God," she whispered.

The enormous insects were coming fast, aiming straight for her and the dog.

"Shit!"

She ran for the tree-line, shouting Lou's name as she went. Together, woman and canine sprinted as fast as feet and paws could carry them, the sound of the drone growing louder with every second.

They hit the woods and kept going, leaping over felled trees and around small boulders, Rebecca not daring a glance back as she used her arms to protect her face from protruding branches.

Not used to running, she mentally cursed herself for not being in better physical condition as her lungs began to burn, but she forced herself onward.

A mere five minutes after entering the forest, she was forced to skid to a stop.

A short distance before them, the forest ended.

Looking straight ahead, then left, then right, she saw there was nothing there. The forest was gone and in its place was a enormous crevasse-a hole that must have been miles wide in every direction.

Rebecca couldn't have guessed how many miles-her spatial awareness had never been that keen, but she knew it had to be several, at least. She'd seen lakes smaller than this canyon.

The flying monstrosities forgotten, Rebecca stood panting, staring at the new topography of her surroundings. Dozens of one-hundred foot pines still slid down the muddy embankments towards the black bottom of the canyon, along with stones, logs and other wild brush.

Remembering her earlier encounter with what now seemed like a miniscule sinkhole, she dared not get to close to the edge and once again, insisted that Lou remain at her side.

"This is not good, boy," she whispered, leaning over to stroke the dog's back.

The canyon was probably a few hundred feet deep but, never particularly fond of heights, Rebecca didn't care to inspect its depth any more than she could its width.

When her awe had subsided somewhat, she started to turn away, but a peculiar movement on the left wall of the canyon caught her eye.

Squinting, she was able to make out another of those insects clawing its way up the wall, causing minor mud avalanches in its wake. Every few seconds, the thing-was it a *bee*?-fluttered its wings in an attempt to fly, but the weight of the mud covering it seemed to be hampering its efforts.

*Those things must be coming out of the ground*, Rebecca thought. *Out of the holes.*

Further inspection proved her theory a moment later when she saw several other creatures attempting the same maneuver. As she watched, one of the things *did* manage to free itself and took flight, thankfully buzzing off in the opposite direction of where she stood with her dog.

"We have to get to town," she muttered. If those things were bees-and they sure as hell looked like they were, though they appeared to have some sort of hard shell-like wings-they were almost certainly dangerous. She supposed anything that large would be dangerous, stinger or not.

She resisted the urge to wonder too much about what they really were, how they came to be or where they were coming from. There would be time for that later, when she was safe.

*If you ever* get *safe.*

Debating on her next course of action left her somewhat stymied. It was hard to move when you knew the ground might disappear from under your feet at any second.

Should they continue to travel through the woods or go back to the road? The road would be easier and faster but she was worried about the bee-like creatures. Out there they would be more vulnerable, though in reality, she doubted the forest was much safer, especially with those things making their way out of the newborn canyon.

Signing, she decided on the road and started back that way, hoping the insects they'd seen had flown along on their merry way to...where?

They were going in the direction of town, same as her.

Rebecca groaned, but what choice did she have? She couldn't go back to her house and she sure as hell couldn't stay here. Town was the only place where she might find shelter and, maybe even better, answers.

After walking only a few dozen yards, Lou froze, lower his head and growled. Rebecca stopped, following his gaze with her own.

Off to the right, maybe twenty feet away, one of the gigantic insects perched on the trunk of a tree about ten feet off the ground. From where she stood, Rebecca could see its antenna twitching and for a moment she feared her bladder would let loose.

Lou growled louder, then barked.

She bit back a scream and crouched beside the dog, grabbing his muzzle in both of her hands.

"Quiet," she hissed.

The dog thrashed his head back and forth in an attempt to get loose, but Rebecca held tight and gave his head a firm shake. "*Quiet*!"

After that, Lou stopped struggling but continued to growl deep in his throat.

When she was sure that he wouldn't bark again, she released his muzzle and took hold of his collar instead, dragging him behind an ancient, moss-covered blue spruce. She stayed crouched low, peering around the tree trunk to get another glimpse at the creature, but by the time she looked, it was already gone.

# CHAPTER 4

The tapping/scratching sound of insect feet on the other side of the glass was nearly enough to make Joe shriek like a little girl.

Slowly, he backed up a few steps, nearly colliding with Stacy who had come forward, her nose wrinkled in disgust as she gaped at the monster bee.

"What the fuck is that?" she asked, grabbing Joe's upper arm, a lit cigarette dangling from the corner of her mouth.

Joe shook his head, unable to speak.

The thing was crawling around out there, tap, tap, tapping against the window, exploring, so large it blocked the outside view of the world through that particular pane.

Occasionally, it fluttered its black wings without taking off, the way insects will sometimes do.

Stacy released Joe's arm and moved even closer to the window, her face full of repulsion, but also a kind of childlike wonder.

"Don't!" Joe clasped her shoulder, halting her

progression to the window.

"*I need a cell phone!*" John screamed from within the kitchen. "*Where is the fucking phone?*"

The man was clearly on the verge of panic, if not there already, and his voice was nearly as grating as the sound of the insect outside, but he reminded Joe of calling the sheriff, which now seemed more important than ever.

"You said your phone's in your coat," he said quietly to Stacy. "Go call the sheriff, quick."

Without looking at him, she asked, "What are you gonna do?"

"I'm getting the shotgun."

They both sprang into action, hurrying away from the front of the diner.

For years, Joe had kept an ancient, double-barreled shotgun in the kitchen. He'd never had to use it before, but it had once belonged to his father, so he kept it clean and in good condition. It was mainly only around for show, though just the employees knew it was there.

The thought of pointing it at anything made his stomach churn, but he pulled it out from behind the dry-goods storage bins and began to rifle through the bins themselves in search of shells. Once located, he loaded up the shotgun, snapped it closed and turned to see John staring at him, wild-eyed.

"You're gonna kill that thing?" the man asked, pointing towards the dining area. "You should go kill it before it gets inside."

"It's not gonna get inside, man." Joe tried to sound calm, though he felt anything but. "This is just a precaution."

At the far end of the kitchen, Stacy removed the phone from her ear and said, "It just keeps ringing. No one picks up."

With his free hand, Joe rubbed the stubble on his cheek and upper lip, then paused, his hand still covering his mouth.

"What do we do now?" Stacy asked.

Before Joe could reply, John lunged at her, snatching the phone from her hand.

"Hey!" Joe protested, taking a step towards the man.

"Watch it!" Stacy snapped, swatting at John as he moved away, head bent as he dialed the phone. "You could ask, you know!"

John ignored them both, pressed send and ran a hand through his grimy hair as he listened to something on the other end of the phone. "Fuck!" he shouted after a moment. "Fucking voicemail!"

He tried dialing again, with the same result. "She should be home right now!" He yelled to no one in particular. "Where the fuck is she?"

Joe shoved his way past John to look out into the dining area again. Their visitor still remained on the window, though except for its antennas, it wasn't moving.

Coming up beside him, Stacy repeated her question: "What are we gonna do, Joe?"

"I don't know," he admitted. "I'm definitely not crazy about going outside right now. What if there are more of those things?"

"So...we just bide our time?"

He shrugged. "I guess so. Unless you have a better idea."

Stacy's eyes remained fixed on the giant insect, both hands rubbing her gently curving belly. Joe was pretty sure she wasn't even aware she was doing it.

"*Motherfucker!*" John shouted, throwing the cell phone as hard as he could against a wall. The device shattered and fell to the floor in several pieces.

"You son-of-a-bitch!" Joe nearly dropped the shotgun, but managed to place it on the counter before whirling and grabbing hold of the front of John's shirt. "What the hell is wrong with you? That was our only phone!"

"*Where is my wife?*" John screamed into Joe's face, as if he really expected Joe to know the answer.

"You're paying for that," Stacy said angrily as she tried to gather up the pieces of her phone. "You prick. There's no way anyone will be able to fix this."

Joe shoved John away and pointed a meaty finger in the other man's face. "You need to calm yourself right now, asshole! I'll toss you out of here in a second if you don't chill the fuck out."

"With that thing out there?" John cried, pointing towards the window. "You don't even know what it is! It could kill me!"

"Yeah, it probably could," Joe agreed. "All the more reason for you to cut the hysteria shit."

Tossing the remnants of her broken phone aside, Stacy changed the subject. "Joe, whatever happened to that old transistor radio you used to have in here?"

Suddenly, Joe's eyes lit up with hope, his altercation with John forgotten. He smiled and said, "I ought to kiss you."

"You wish, old man."

Together, they began rummaging around the kitchen, searching for the radio while John circled around to the other side of the counter and began pacing back and forth, sweat running down his temples as his hands gestured wildly, though his mutterings were inaudible.

"Got it," Stacy announced, pulling the radio out of a lower stainless steel cupboard. She scowled as she studied it. "Jesus, when did you buy this? 1966?"

"Funny," Joe said, taking the radio from her and

twisting the power knob. Immediately, static blared from the tinny speaker and Joe hurried to turn down the volume as Stacy clasped her hands over her ears.¶He looked up, his smile ever broader. "Batteries still work."

"That's a minor miracle," Stacy said, though she returned his smile.

Joe put the radio on the counter, stretched its antenna and began spinning the tuning dial in search of anything other than static. It took nearly a full minute of barely moving the knob, but finally the crackle of a distant voice could be heard.

"Right there!" Stacy said.

"I know!"

They both stared at the radio, straining to heard the male voice which sounded so far away it might have been coming from another planet.

"...*complete devastation...no estimations...deaths...*"

John leaned over the counter. "Make it come in clearer!"

In unison, Joe and Stacy shushed him.

"*...gone...*"

"What's gone?" John demanded.

Joe shot him a dirty look. "Shut the hell up."

"*...approximately 250 miles...growing...*"

"250 miles?" John asked. "What the fuck are they talking about?"

Opening her mouth to yell at him, Stacy was interrupted as a deafening explosion rocked the building, shaking loose anything that wasn't nailed down, including pans, cutlery, small appliances, condiments and half a dozen other things. All three of them instinctively ducked, covering their heads as the power went out and plunged them into dimness.

Plaster rained down on them from the ceiling and a

wall clock crashed to the floor with the sound of breaking glass.

When he was certain it was safe, Joe dropped his arms and looked around, dazed.

"That was close by," Stacy said, straightening up. "Probably a block away at most."

"Yeah," Joe agreed. "I'm gonna take a look out the back door."

"NO!" Stacy shouted, stepping in front of him. "I don't think that's a good idea."

"We have to know what happened. Someone could be hurt."

"And that someone could be you if you go out there."

"I'm just gonna have a peek. I promise."

"But...that *thing*."

"It's gone," John said, gaping towards the front of the diner.

Joe and Stacy both looked and saw that he was correct. The bee-or whatever it was-was no longer on the window.

"Huh," Joe said. "The explosion must have scared it off."

Stacy cocked her head, listening. "We should hear sirens pretty soon. The fire department is only a couple miles away."

"I'm not waiting for the fire department," Joe said, seizing his shotgun. When Stacy tried to block his way again, he said, "If I see anything that ain't...right...I'll blast it. Okay?"

"No," she snapped. "It's not okay. Something happens to you and I'm in here alone with..." She waved at John with disgust.

"Just a *peek*," he repeated firmly, pushing past her.

Throwing her hands into the air with exasperation,

Stacy cursed and began searching the floor for her cigarettes. When she couldn't find them, she quickly spun around and called after Joe. "Fuck it. I want a peek too."

He knew better than to argue with her anymore. Instead, he said, "Just stay behind me."

"Don't you worry about that," she said, one hand against her tummy. "Junior here is gonna be pressed right up against your ass."

Joe was amazed at her ability to retain some of her humor in this fucked-up situation and he had to admire her for it. God knew he wasn't in the mood for jokes. In fact, if he was being honest with himself, he knew he was damn close to pissing his pants.

They went through the doorway and into the storage room where the backdoor was located. Moving into deeper gloom, he wished he'd grabbed a flashlight from the kitchen, but knew as soon as they reached the door to the outside they'd have all the light they needed.

Luckily, they'd both spent enough time back here that they could have maneuvered blindfolded and neither of them bumped into anything.

Once they reached the door, Joe gripped the knob with his free hand and glanced over his shoulder at Stacy.

"Ready?"

Her shadow nodded, barely visible, and Joe blinked sweat out of his eyes. Fuck! Why was he so scared?

Taking a deep, steadying breath, he turned the knob and slowly opened the door a crack. Sunlight streamed into the room, temporarily blinding him.

Joe squinted, peeking through the opening. In the distance, the blue sky was smeared with black and the smoke cloud was rolling towards the Pinecone Cafe.

"See anything?" Stacy asked.

"The explosion wasn't as close as we thought. Maybe

half a mile. I'd say it might have been the 7-11 up the road. Close to it, anyway." He paused, studying the smoke. "But judging the way that wind is blowing, that smoke is gonna be over us in about ten minutes."

"What about the monster bug? Is that out there?"

Joe shook his head. "Not that I can see." He opened the door further and braved poking his head outside, looking around. To his left, the normally busy road was completely deserted. The right was somewhat obscured due to the Dumpster he kept back there, but from what he could see, there was nothing out of the ordinary. Behind the diner's paved surface was just the lip of the forest and it was too dark to see anything of interest in there.

"Seems safe enough," he said. "I want to see if I can get a better look."

Ignoring Stacy's protest, he swung the door wide and prepared to venture outside, shotgun at the ready.

"*Stop!*" John shouted as he raced into the room, causing both Joe and Stacy to jump and whirl around.

John held the transistor radio in his hand. It only took Joe a moment to realize the man was crying.

"I heard them," John wept. "They said Seattle is gone. Just...gone. It sunk. The whole fucking thing."

Joe let the door fall closed, casting them into blackness.

"But..." Stacy began. "How is that possible?"

"That's not all I heard either," John sniffed. "Those...bees...or whatever the fuck they are. They're attacking people. They're fucking killing them!"

Neither Joe nor Stacy spoke, shocked into silence, but the radio crackled in the dark and the faraway voice told them that the end had come.

# CHAPTER 5

The Day house stood on a large piece of property but could still be easily seen from the road.

Rebecca was relieved to see it was still standing as she neared it. Along the way, she'd encountered several more sinkholes, though none nearly as large as the one which had taken out acres upon acres of forest. A few had been bigger than a typical swimming pool and twice as deep but as far as she could tell nothing had been emerging from them.

She had seen several more of the bee-like creatures while she traveled. Most of them had been in flight and each time Rebecca had hidden, dragging her dog with her.

With the exception of the huge insects and the trees, she had seen nothing alive and it was this fact, more than any other that had come before it, which gave her a foreboding sense of doom. The world had gone too quiet and the possibility that she and Lou were the only ones left alive tickled at her brain like the tiny, scuttling legs of a black spider.

Walking up the Day's dirt driveway, she saw what

looked at first like a bundle of laundry on the lawn near the front porch. Frowning, she turned her attention to the brown Land Rover in the drive, its driver's side door standing open.

"Martin?" she called as she drew closer to the vehicle. "Joyce?"

When she reached the Rover, she peered inside only to find it empty. She noted that the keys were in the ignition, though the auto wasn't running.

*Odd*, she thought.

Lou pushed past her and leapt into the vehicle, panting at her from the passenger's seat.

Rebecca considered scolding him, but decided against it. What would be the purpose at this point? Instead, she said, "Sorry, buddy. No rides today."

Turning to face the house, Rebecca felt a small surge of hope. The fact that the Land Rover was here meant that the Days were home. That seemed like a good sign, despite the silence. In fact, Joyce was probably peeking out from behind a curtained window at her at this very moment, busy-body that she was.

"Come on, boy," she said and began her way across the lawn to the front door.

She was about forty feet from the bundle on the ground when she realized it wasn't laundry at all.

Gasping, she broke into a run, Lou at her heels.

When she reached the body of Joyce Day, she skidded to a halt and bit into the knuckle of her index finger to keep from screaming.

The elderly woman had been dead for some time, judging by the flies swarming around her. Her face was completely gone, as was most of the exposed flesh of her arms and legs-anything not covered by her flower-print house dress.

What from a distance Rebecca had thought was various pieces of red garments, was actually raw, red meat, oozing blood, a stark-white protrusion of bone here and there.

Joyce Day now resembled a freshly butchered carcass wearing a dress, black orthopedic shoes and a curly gray wig.

Sniffing cautiously, the dog inspected the corpse from every angle, disturbing the feast of the flies while Rebecca stepped back a pace, fighting the urge to retch.

*What could have done this?* But she already knew the answer, if only because there was no other. Those *things*...those bee creatures.

The realization made her check her surroundings; she searched the blue sky for any sign of movement, her ears pricked for that now familiar high-pitched drone.

She saw nothing but it didn't make her feel any safer. Knowing how fast the things could fly, one could be upon her long before she could outrun it.

A chill racked her body and turned her attention to the house. Martin must be inside, probably hiding, paralyzed with terror and surely traumatized by the killing of his wife.

Rebecca stepped around the body, trying not to think about the flies, some of which were probably already laying eggs in the savaged flesh of the old woman.

She climbed the porch steps quickly, anxious to find Martin but also to get inside where it would be safe from enormous and apparently carnivorous insects.

The inside of the house was dark, all the curtains drawn tight and from somewhere within it, Rebecca could hear the ticking of a grandfather clock, each swing of the pendulum as loud as a firecracker in a long-abandoned crypt.

"Martin?" she called, deciding to leave the front door open behind her. "It's Rebecca Robinson. Hello?"¶From where she stood in the foyer, the living room was directly to her right. A quick scan told her the room was empty and she moved down the hall to the kitchen and dining area, only to find these places were also void of life.

After checking the bathroom as well as the screened-in back porch to no avail, she was left with the upper level of the house.

Standing at the foot of the stairs, she swallowed, her palms suddenly moist with perspiration.

Could he be sleeping? And if so, for how long? Did he even know his wife was dead?¶Rebecca shook her head. The feeling of impending doom was almost enough to make her flee the house entirely, but where would she go? Into town, of course, but to what end?¶She couldn't think about that now.

Briefly, she considered forgoing the search for Martin and just heading back to the kitchen to use their telephone and call for help.

She looked down at Lou, faithfully standing beside her, gazing up at her with adoring eyes and a gently swaying tail. "What do you say, boy? Up or just get the hell out?"

Lou's only response was a soft whine.

"I was afraid you'd say that. Up it is, I guess."

For the first time since entering the house, she felt like an intruder and proceeded slowly, her hand trailing along the mahogany rail, each riser creaking underfoot.

The dog had no such qualms. He raced by her as if he were in his own house, making it to the top of the stairs in a few quick seconds.

On the landing, Lou turned to look down at Rebecca as if pleased with himself, then darted away, out of sight.

"Lou!" Rebecca hissed, increasing her pace. She imagined the dog scaring the crap out of poor old Mr. Day and winced inwardly.

"Martin?" she called again as she crested the stairs. "I'm sorry. It's me, Rebecca, from up the road."

In another room, Lou barked once and she hurried towards the sound.

The second level of the house was even darker than the first but she made it to a far bedroom at the end of the hall without banging into anything.

She stopped at the threshold of the master bedroom, waiting for her eyes to adjust to the gloom.

"Martin?"

When black shapes formed into actual objects-bed, dresser, hope chest-she saw her neighbor seated in an armchair by the window facing the front lawn. He appeared to be gazing out the window, though the blind was barely cracked.

At his feet, Lou sat, watching the man expectantly, his tail thumping the carpet.

Rebecca swallowed what felt like a cantaloupe lodged in her throat. Martin didn't move, didn't acknowledge either the dog or herself.

The most disturbing part of the scene was the rifle laying across the old man's lap.

"You saw what the bastards did to Joyce."

The man's words so startled Rebecca that she cried out, clasping a hand to her mouth.

Finally Martin turned his head to look at her. "You saw it, Rebecca?"

She nodded as her heart pounded painfully against her breastbone. "Yes."

"It's over now. You know that, dontcha?"

Crossing the room, she sat on the edge of the bed

nearest the old man and leaned over, placing a hand on his knee, doing her best to ignore the rifle so casually placed on his thighs.

"Those...creatures," she said. "One of them did that to Joyce?"

"Digger bees," he said.

Brow furrowed, she said, "Excuse me?"

"Those creatures. I've seen something like 'em before. Those are digger bees, sure as shit."

"I've...I've never heard of digger bees before."

"They live in the ground. Where they get their name from. They dig their nests in the ground 'stead of building 'em like regular bees. Stepped on a nest once when I was a boy down in Oregon. Bastards can be fierce. Foot swelled up the size of a damn football." He chuckled a bit at the memory, then continued. "'Course never saw any so big. That part I don't know about. Probably some science project gone awry or some crap they been putting in the soil or water supply. Poison, probably. Who knows, right? Don't matter now anyway."

Rebecca thought about this for a moment, then said, "But...since when do bees..." She trailed off, grateful for the dark because it prevented Martin from seeing her blush. "Do what they did to Joyce?" she finished.

"They ate her," Martin said, matter-of-factly. "That's what they did to her. Goddamn me having this rifle locked up in the attic. Might have been able to save her if I wasn't so damn worried the grandkids might find it in the closet sometime when I was watching a game or some shit. Goddamn me all to hell."

Straightening her back, she said, "I always thought bees just...pollinated flowers and mostly minded their own business. I didn't think they ate..."

"Meat?" he asked. "You ever had a picnic in the park?

44

Damn yellow jackets seem like they'll eat just about anything, if you let them. Same thing here, I suppose. I reckon we're the flowers now. What else they gonna pollinate? And as far as minding their own business. Well, I don't know what to say about that one. That bastard that came after my wife...he was an aggressive son-of-a-bitch." He seemed to ponder than for a moment before continuing. "'Course Joyce wasn't just standing there either. Treated the damn thing like she would any other flying pest, waving her arms around trying to swat it. Screamin' like the dickens. Probably aggravated it. And there I was, a useless old bum, running for the house and telling her to stay still and quiet." He shook his head sadly. "Fat lotta good that did. By the time I got back with the rifle, she was on the ground and she wasn't moving. That bastard was on top of her and I could..." His voice hitched and it took a few seconds for him to go on. "I could see its damn jaws working on her...face. It was already eating her face, Rebecca!"

The man burst into tears and Rebecca said nothing. She didn't know how to console someone who had gone through so a horrific ordeal or even if such a person *could* be consoled. Certainly not so soon after the fact anyway.

Martin produced a handkerchief from a shirt pocket and blew his nose loudly.

When she thought the worst of his crying might have passed, Rebecca asked, "So, you shot it?"

He cleared his throat. "Tried to. Missed the damn thing by a mile I was shakin' so bad. Guess the round was close enough for the bastard to feel its breeze though, 'cause it took off after that." He blew his nose again. "But, they keep coming back every twenty minutes or so. Taking small bites outta my wife. Seems they like they taste of her. The soft, juicy bits."

Rebecca closed her eyes and mentally begged Martin to stop with his narrative. Her stomach churned and if he said much more, she would surely gag and she knew for certain where *that* would lead.

"I didn't bother to take another shot," Martin went on. "What would be the point? She's dead and at this rate, there won't be much to bury anyway. But I'm still keeping an eye out, just in case."

From where he'd curled up on the floor, Lou whined softly, almost as if he'd fallen asleep and was having a nightmare. Rebecca supposed it was possible. She was bone-tired and the dog probably was as well.

"Been going out to the Rover to listen to the radio," Martin said. "Couldn't hear much but I heard enough. I did that a few times, until I didn't want to hear anymore."

Rebecca asked what he *had* heard, and when he was done telling her, she knew how he felt. She didn't want to hear anymore either.

A sinkhole just slightly smaller than the Grand Canyon had opened up, stretching from just north of Seattle, all the way down to Portland, Oregon. Millions were dead.

And apparently the canyon was growing, opening wider, stretching longer. In addition, other, smaller sinkholes were forming and soon, it was guessed, the small ones would connect with the new canyon until the majority of the northwest seaside of the United States would be swallowed whole.

"You need to start traveling east, Rebecca," Martin told her. "Go east as fast as you can and don't look back."

The small crack of light sneaking in from between the curtains was already starting to wane. It got dark early this time of year.

"Well, what are we waiting for then?" Rebecca stood up. "Let's go."

Lou, ever obedient, jumped to his feet, ready for the next adventure. Martin, however, remained seated.

"Oh, hell, no," he said. "I'm too old to be running from monsters digging their way up outta Hell. I'm just gonna sit here and wait."

"Wait for what?"

"For another one of those bastards to come and try to take another bite outta my wife!" He sounded angry now and shook his head. "I've been sitting here, watching 'em. Studyin' them, I guess you could say. I just want to take out one. Just one and I'll be happy. As God as my witness, I won't miss a second time."

Rebecca tried arguing with him, but it was of no use. She couldn't force the man to come with her, though she sorely wanted him to. She was terrified of going anywhere alone and voiced this fear to him, to no avail.

"Take whatever you can carry from my refrigerator. And take my Rover," he said. "It's a good truck and it'll take you wherever you need to go." He gave the dog an absentminded pat on the head. "As long as there are roads, anyway."

Not wanting to cry, Rebecca thanked him and got out of there fast. She didn't stop in the kitchen, though she thought she probably should. But she didn't want to take anything Martin might need himself.

When she was just about to the front door, he called down to her one last time. "Godspeed, Rebecca! May the good Lord bless us all."

She was about to respond when the crack of the rifle shattered the otherwise quiet house. Flinching, she looked out the doorway to the lawn, expecting to see one of the huge digger bees, dead or alive, but there was nothing. Either Martin had missed again...or he hadn't.

# CHAPTER 6

As odd as it seemed, more than anything, Joe wanted a beer. It was strange, he thought, the things you think of when you don't expect to live through the night.

They'd continued to listen to the radio as afternoon bled into evening and more of the creatures came and went. It seemed there must have been thousands of them now and Joe was afraid that the time to escape the diner had long since dissipated.

After a while, he had decided to take stock of their supplies, feeling somewhat lucky to have been at work at the time the shit hit the fan. By his estimation, they would probably be okay food-wise for a couple of weeks, if it came to that.

That was, if the bee creatures didn't bust their way inside first.

Stacy had remained stoic as the drone of the monsters grew more steady, but John was becoming increasingly hysterical with every passing hour. His panic became ever more exacerbated when they began hearing choppers flying overhead. Too terrified to go outside, he began screaming for help through the back door, which he dared not open more than a crack.

"They're not gonna hear you!" Joe yelled at the other man, grabbing him by the shoulder. "Even if you were on the goddamn roof they wouldn't hear you!"

John stopped his screaming to look at Joe. "Yes! he said. "We need to get to the roof! Even if they can't hear us, they'll at least see us!"

"Maybe, maybe not."

"You have the shotgun! You'll be safe. Just shoot those bastards if they get too close!"

Joe bit back his anger. "You think I should be the one to risk my ass, huh?"

"Well...why not? It's your diner. It's your fucking gun. You act like you're so fucking macho, why don't you prove it?"

"It's better if we just stay put for now," Joe said, ignoring the taunts. "At least until we haven't seen or heard any of those things for a while."

"It's getting worse not better!" John screamed, spittle flying through the darkness to shower Joe's face. "We have to do something *now*!"

"You're free to do what you want, man," Joe said. He tossed his hands in the air and turned his back on John, shaking his head.

A distant rumble shook the diner and was followed by an explosion. Both were far enough away to not pose any immediate danger to the diner but the sounds were unnerving nonetheless. It told them all that the earth had swallowed more evidence of mankind and most probably took lives down with it.

Behind Joe, John began to cry again.

Fresh out of sympathy, Joe said "Don't open that door unless I'm here." Without turning, he walked out of the storage room and back into the kitchen which was now aglow with weak candlelight.

At the counter, Stacy sat toying with an unlit cigarette. Her face was drawn; she looked as though she'd aged at least a decade in a matter of hours. Joe guessed he probably looked the same.

He nodded at the cigarette. "You gonna smoke that?"

Stacy signed. "I never wanted this baby," she said softly, without looking up at him. "But I don't believe in abortion either, so I figured I was just fucked. Thought I might put it up for adoption, you know?"

Joe shifted his weight uncomfortably and said nothing.

"But now," she continued. "I'm thinking maybe I do want it after all. I'm thinking about what a selfish bitch I've been, smoking these cancer sticks. I even kept right on smoking a little weed now and then. Drinking. I didn't really give a fuck. I was pissed off." Her voice hitched and Joe reached across the counter to clasp her left hand.

"So stupid," she said. "I've been so fucking stupid." She sniffed loudly, then straightened her back. "I turned the radio off. Figured I'd save the batteries since there's been nothing back static for about an hour now."

"Good thinking," Joe said, because he didn't know what else to say.

"We should have left earlier," she said. "While it was still daylight. I have a feeling this..." She finally brought her gaze up to look him in the eye. "This is probably gonna be our last night. I'm really starting to think we're not gonna get out of this."

Joe frowned. "Yes, we are. Don't think like that. Yeah, I guess we probably should have left when everything started going to hell but how were we to know things would..." He trailed off, remembering John's words. *It's getting worse not better.* After letting go of Stacy's hand, he said, "You should get some rest. We'll find some stuff to make you up a little bed on the floor away from the doors and windows. How's that sound?"

She snatched a paper napkin from the nearest dispenser and blew her nose. When she was finished, she said, "I think I'd rather be awake."

He nodded. He couldn't blame her. As exhausted as he was, he didn't think he'd have been able to sleep. Maybe later, but not now.

"What are we gonna do, Joe?"

"I don't know," he admitted. "But we need a plan. I think we've been lucky so far but waiting around for a rescue that may never come is probably not the way we should play it for much longer."

Stacy studied her unlit cigarette thoughtfully for a moment before turning her attention to the ceiling. "Do you hear that?"

Joe listened. All he could hear was John weeping in the back room. "What?"

"Nothing."

"Oh." He turned away, intending to go check on John again.

"No," she said. "I mean, literally, *nothing*. I don't hear that buzzing sound anymore."

Cocking his head, Joe discovered that Stacy was right. For the first time in hours, the constant drone of the insects travelling back and forth outside had stopped. "Maybe they all flew away?" he suggested.

"Or maybe they went to sleep."

Joe chuckled half-heartedly.

"I'm serious," Stacy said. "How often do you see bees at night? They really do sleep."

He had to admit she had a point. "So...we might be able to get out of here."

Stacy nodded. "Maybe. We should at least take a look around."

They crossed the diner to the front windows and peered out, though it was hard to see anything at all beyond their own cars.

"It's too dark," Stacy said. "But as far as I can tell, nothing's moving."

"We should check out back, too."

It seemed silly, but at least it gave them a purpose for the moment.

He retrieved the shotgun from where he'd put it at the far end of the counter and together they went back into the storage room, Stacy wielding the flashlight.

John was slumped on the floor, his back against the outside door, his knees drawn up to his chest with his arms wrapped around his legs and his head down.

"Gotta move, buddy," Joe told him. "We need to take another look out back."

Without bothering to lift his head, John asked, "What for?"

"We think those things might be gone," Stacy told him. She sounded cautiously hopeful and Joe was glad for that, at least. "If they are, maybe we can get out of here."

"And go where?" Despite his voice being muffled, it was clear that John was still pissed. Joe wondered if he'd always been pissed and this was just the latest drama in the younger man's life.

"Just get up," Joe told him.

John raised his head and squinted into the glare of Stacy's flashlight. "My wife is dead. What the fuck do I care what happens now?"

Joe was about to explode but Stacy spoke first.

"You don't know that," she said. "And even if she is, *you* aren't."

"I may as well be."

Slowly, Joe said, "Move your ass or I'll move it for you."

Face darkening, John snapped, "Fuck you! This is the stupidest fucking thing-"

Joe leveled the shotgun at him. "*Now!*"

John rose to his feet quickly, though not out of fear-out of anger. "Oh, you're gonna shoot me?" he shouted. "Go for it! You'll be doing me a fucking favor!"

Despite not looking at her, Joe could sense Stacy's eyes on him and her tension. He lowered the weapon and forced himself to speak calmly. "Thank you."

"*Motherfucker!*" John spat as Joe brushed by him to open the door. "Fucking point a gun at me!"

Disregarding the younger man, Joe said, "Stacy, come over here with that flashlight."

She did as asked, crouching down beside Joe who had opened the door wide enough to fit half his body through, leading with the weapon.

The beam of light pierced the night and Stacy slowly swung it in all directions, taking care to shine it back towards the woods behind the diner.

"I don't see anything," she whispered.

"Me neither."

"I bet we could make it to one of the cars now," she added.

"Probably safer on foot. We don't want to be driving and hit one of those sinkholes."

Behind them, John barked out a loud, phony laugh. "Oh, you don't think so, Joe? You know a lot about it, don't ya?

In unison, Joe and Stacy hissed "*SHHH!*"

"Get the fuck out of the way!" John charged forward and grabbed a fistful of Stacy's hair, yanking her backwards until her balance was lost and she went sprawling to the floor. The beam from the flashlight caused light and shadows to dance around the small storage room, producing a disorienting effect.

"*Hey!*" Joe shouted, spinning towards John, the shotgun in one hand while the other curled into a fist and reared back, preparing to strike.

John was quick however, and darted to one side, the blow glancing off his shoulder and not slowing him down in the slightest. He used his body weight to shove Joe backwards into a shelving unit. Joe managed to remain upright and not lose his grip on the shotgun but by the time he recovered, John was already out the door, racing through the back lot towards the street.

"*JOHN!*" Stacy screeched, much too late, as she stumbled to her feet and caught the door before it could swing closed. "*Come back!*"

John skidded to a stop and whirled around, tears streaming down his face. "All clear," he shouted deliriously, throwing his arms into the air. "Not a fucking thing in-"

A large, dark shape, barely visible in the night, came over the roof of the diner and whizzed through the air. The drone was unmistakable.

Stacy screamed as the huge bee thing crashed into John, knocking him back a good ten feet, the two of them-creature and man-rolling across the tarmac in a blur.

"Shit!" Joe shouted, lunging out the door himself, shotgun raised as he ran towards John.

"*Joe! No!*" Stacy bellowed.

Stopping, Joe tried to take aim at the creature, but he was unable to get a clear shot. He was at least twenty feet away but even in the dark that still plenty close enough to see the bee on top of John curl its rear end and the long, dripping stinger plunge into John's abdomen.

John shrieked loud enough to crack the night as Joe ran right up to the two of them and placed the muzzle of the shotgun against the bee's body and pulled the trigger.

The bee creature exploded, torn nearly in half, spraying both John and Joe with a foul smelling slime that was hot to the touch. Hot enough to burn, though Joe barely noticed this fact, shouting, "*Yes!*" at the dead creature.

The victory was short-lived, as another dark shadow flew in from the direction of the street and as he spun to face it, piercing light blinded him and he raised his free arm to shield his eyes.

At his feet, John continued to wail.

# CHAPTER 7

Rebecca had been cruising slowly down 99th with the Land Rover's headlights off when she saw the man get attacked by one of the digger bees.

It was a minor miracle that she'd been able to see anything at all in the dark, and probably wouldn't have seen the man at all, but she saw the bee first, perched on the roof of the Pinecone Cafe.

In her sluggish travels across town, she had learned two things about the bees: they were attracted to light and sound, the latter of which seemed to agitate them greatly.

She had learned both of these the hard way, the vehicle having been attacked no less than three times since she'd driven it out of Martin's driveway.

The attacks, though frightening, had proved fruitless on the creatures' part though. They were unable to get inside the Rover and once Rebecca had stifled her own urge to scream and the dog's frantic barking, the things had eventually flown away. She'd had to kill the engine multiple times during her journey because the sound of it brought them towards it more often than not and despite them not being able to get at her, she still didn't want to be swarmed.

And she'd seen swarms.

Dozens of the digger bees had descended upon a Wal-Mart parking lot, bouncing off the lamp posts the way moths will bounce against a porch light.

She had kept the vehicle at a crawl, lights off, until she was a good four blocks from the Wal-Mart and had since seen other examples of the bees being drawn to light and sound.

So far, she'd seen very few people alive out on the streets and suspected that most folks had either fled early on or were hiding inside their homes. There were a lot of car wrecks along the way, mostly one-vehicle accidents, and she assumed the drivers had panicked when they'd been attacked by the flying monstrosities, crashing their cars and either escaping when they could or remaining inside, out of sight or injured.

Creeping along the road, she'd heard a man shouting and grimaced inwardly, knowing exactly what that would mean if he was out in the open and then, sure enough, she'd seen movement and, tracking the bee, she'd seen the man arms reaching skyward.

Her first thought was that he'd been *trying* to attract a bee, though why anyone would do such a thing, she couldn't imagine. Then the bee had struck him and another man rushed out of the diner, also shouting.

Rebecca swerved the Rover into the lot and flipped the headlights on, hoping to draw the bee off the fallen man and to her. She hit the brakes hard just as a loud *crack* blasted the night.

The standing man spun to look at her and she immediately saw he held a rifle of some sort. Cursing, she instinctively ducked below the dashboard, fully expecting her windshield to explode.

Instead, she heard more yelling and then the man with the weapon was at the driver's side window, beating it with the side of his fist.

In the backseat, Lou began to go ballistic, barking and snarling, obviously terrified.

"Stop it!" Rebecca shouted at the man. "You'll bring them right to you!"

But her warning was too late as another bee smacked hard into the man, pinning him against the door of the Rover, its mandibles snapping inches from the back of his head.

Rebecca's eyes met the man's for an instant and then his own eyes screwed closed in agony.

*He's being stung!*

It was below her line of vision, but she knew it was happening.

She felt like screaming herself, completely helpless and horrified as this man was killed right in front of her with only a car window between them.

*"GET OFF OF HIM, YOU FUCKING PRICK!"*

Rebecca blinked in surprise as a shrieking woman came running at the vehicle brandishing a baseball bat and clubbing at the enormous insect with all her might.

The woman hit the thing over and over, until it fell away from the man, perhaps stunned, and onto the ground. The man slumped out of sight as well and Rebecca's paralysis broke.

She unlocked and opened the door and shouted at the young woman. "*Get inside!*"

The woman ignored her, kneeling at the man's side. "Joe? Joe! Are you okay?"

"My...leg..." the man groaned. "Bastard got me."

A deafening crunch came from the direction of the

diner, snatching Rebecca's attention away from the strangers for a moment. The entire building shifted and then the far side collapsed inward with the sound of splintering wood and crushed metal.

"Oh, God," she whispered. She looked at the two people on the ground and yelled, "Come on! You have to get in here right now! It's not safe! The ground is giving way!"

When the two seemed too dazed to comprehend what she was saying, she leapt out of the vehicle and struggled to get the man to his feet. She opened the Rover's back door and did all but shove him inside. Turning back to the girl, she said, "*HURRY!*"

Finally understanding, the girl climbed into the vehicle and Rebecca slammed the door behind her, jumping in behind the wheel and slamming her own door as well.

Then her eyes fell on the crumpled, unmoving form still in the lot. "What about him?" she asked the young woman.

"He's a dick," the girl replied.

Rebecca probably would have been amused by this response under different circumstances, but now she said only, "Good, because he's dead."

She threw the Rover into reverse and hit the gas, the dog still barking in her ear.

Once she'd pulled back onto the road, she again cut the headlights. Behind them, the diner exploded, probably due to a ruptured gas line.

"*Holy shit!*" the girl cried, covering her head.

"You can say that again," Rebecca said, speeding up. "Lou, *quiet!*"

The dog immediately fell silent and went to work sniffing the moaning man.

"The stinger..." the man said. "Pretty sure it broke off

in my thigh." He was struggling to sit up, teeth gritted against the pain. "Help me get it out, Stacy."

"What?" Stacy asked. "Joe, I..." She began to cry. "I don't know if I can."

"Please," Joe grunted. "If you don't..." He trailed off, wheezing for breath.

Now that they were a safe distance from the diner, Rebecca slowed the vehicle to a crawl. In the rearview mirror she could see the flames shooting into the night sky and some of the bees darting towards it and then away.

"Go on," she growled under her breath. "Get in there you sons-of-bitches. Burn."

In the backseat, Stacy said, "I think I feel it."

Joe fought to get air into his lungs and rasped, "Pull...it...out."

Rebecca winced a moment later when Joe let out a piercing scream. "Got it!" Stacy said triumphantly. "Shit! It's...barbed!"

Catching a glimpse of the stinger in the mirror, Rebecca quickly returned her attention to the road. It was probably two feet long, black and had what appeared to be thorns all along its length. Definitely a nasty bit of work.

Stacy's triumph was brief. "Now you're bleeding. *Shit*!" To Rebecca, she said, "Do you have anything in here we can use to wrap his leg?"

"I don't know," she said apologetically. "This isn't my car. Look around in the back."

Turning in the seat, Stacy rummaged around but all she came up with was a wool blanket and an old blue and tan flannel shirt. She did the best she could with the shirt, binding Joe's upper thigh with before covering him with the blanket. A few hisses of pain escaped through Joe's clenched teeth, but otherwise he was silent through the process.

"There," Stacy said when she was finished. "That should help."

Joe took a long ragged breath and said, "I guess I should mention I'm allergic to bee stings."

Both women gasped, but he lifted a bloody hand to silence them. "All the Benadryl in the world won't help this one. It's a...doozy."

"Jesus," Rebecca whispered.

"We need to get him to a hospital," Stacy said, her voice on the teetering edge of panic. "We need to *go now!*"

Rebecca licked her lips and shook her head slowly. "I've been driving for hours looking for a way out of town. So far, all the roads leading out are gone."

"What do you mean 'gone'?"

"I mean...*gone*. The sinkholes just swallowed them. I haven't been able to find one completely intact yet and nothing's been passable."

Stacy let out a long string of curses then fell silent for a few seconds. "Well..what about that clinic over on Poplar?"

Rebecca thought about it. "I haven't been down that way yet, but I can try taking the long way around." She didn't say what she was really thinking-that it would be a miracle if the clinic was not only standing but operational as well. But, she supposed, what could it hurt to try?

"His face is getting all splotchy!" Stacy said suddenly. "Oh my God, what should I do?" When Rebecca didn't reply, she yelled, "Drive faster!"

Pressing down slightly on the accelerator, Rebecca said, "I can't drive too fast or the bees will come."

"Who cares! Just go!"

"If they come," Rebecca tried to explain patiently,

"then we won't even be able to get your friend out of the car."

Joe's breathing became even more labored and Lou let out a long, low whine. Beside them, Stacy began to cry.

Grim-faced, Rebecca drove on in the direction of the clinic, carefully weaving around abandoned vehicles and the occasional bodies of the dead, both human and otherwise.

# CHAPTER 8

Not only was clinic gone, but the entire northwest corner of town had dissolved into mud, absorbed back into the earth from which it came. What lay beyond the hood of the Rover was a vast black field of empty space, a gorge with no bottom to be seen.

"It's getting worse," Rebecca said. She felt entirely defeated. If Joe was still breathing in the backseat, she couldn't hear him over the soft sound of Stacy's gentle weeping. That fact alone let her know that he probably wasn't.

She put the Rover in reverse and slowly backed away from that vacant space, not daring to let herself think about the lives that must have been lost in the last twenty-four hours.

"My baby," Stacy sobbed. "Oh, God, my poor baby."

Rebecca's heart broke for the young woman as she turned the Rover back in the direction they'd come from. She was about to ask if Stacy had been married to Joe when she felt the back left side of the Rover sink. Both she and Stacy screamed in terror as the land behind the vehicle began to collapse.

Grimacing, Rebecca stomped on the gas pedal, thanking the powers that be for front-wheel-drive and the Rover lurched forward, the back wheel bumping back up onto solid ground.

Stacy spun around to look out the rear window. "Fuck!" she shouted. "Drive! *Drive drive, drive*!"

Behind them, the new gorge was growing, ingesting the ground and everything on it with an insatiable appetite. Despite driving as fast as she could, the earth was disintegrating no more than a car length after they passed over it.

"*SHIIIIIITTTTT!*" Rebecca yelled, gripping the steering wheel with all her might. She was dimly aware of the pandemonium happening behind her, the girl screaming, the dog barking, the earth crumpling into nothingness, but she kept her eyes straight ahead, pushing the Rover on, leaning forward towards the dashboard as if it would make them move faster.

They hadn't gotten far when another crevasse opened up in front of them, smaller than the one behind, but still wide enough to take them down into oblivion.

Rebecca jerked the wheel to the right, going off-road, over a median strip, across a patch of lawn and into a small apartment complex parking lot. Swerving around the building, narrowly avoiding parked cars, they exited the other side onto long abandoned train tracks, the Rover's engine roaring its protest.

Keeping to the tracks, Rebecca didn't dare slow down. Parallel to the tracks, the ground was vanishing on one side while the edge of the forest lay on the other.

"We're so fucking screwed," Stacy said, sounding almost calm now. "So fucking screwed."

From the right, where the forest was, came the sound

that Rebecca had come to know so well: falling trees. Faraway, but certainly not far enough.

"*Come on!*" Rebecca snarled savagely as she saw an opening on the left where there was still a section of ground wide enough to let them pass. The Rover veered that way, its occupants bouncing violently within it, but otherwise silent now.

As soon as she'd made the move, Rebecca saw that it had been a mistake and hit the brakes, causing the Rover to fishtail and throwing both Stacy and the dog forward. They each let out a yelps of pain and fear and then the vehicle was still.

Nothing lay in front of them.

Nothing lay behind or to either side.

The Rover sat on an island of earth, perhaps 84 feet wide and 100 feet in length.

Rebecca had no idea what was holding up this scrap of land, but she was grateful for it, knowing it was not likely to last more than a few minutes at most.

Stacy said nothing, but she didn't cry either. She simply sat looking out the passenger side window, her eyes full of wonder and resignation.

Thinking about Glen, Rebecca sighed and turned to look at her dog. "Come here, Lou," she said and patted her lap. The dog obliged, hopping over the center console to sit on top of his mistress, panting, wearing much the same expression as Stacy wore.

Burying her face in his fur, Rebecca sniffed and murmured, "You're a good boy, Lou. A good boy." She could feel the dog's heart beating strong and steady in his chest and this gave her comfort. "We'll see daddy soon."

When she lifted her face again, the eastern horizon was blushing the palest shade of gray she'd ever seen and the creatures were buzzing back forth in all directions.

Dozens of them, all going about their own mysterious business.

*This is their world now*, she thought.

She hoped somewhere the earth still belonged to people, but in her heart of hearts she suspected that even if it did, it wouldn't be for much longer.

Watching the enormous digger bees, she absently scratched her dog's neck and listened to the hum of a distant chopper flying somewhere over head. The sound gave her a slight twinge of hope, but she knew better. She supposed Stacy knew better as well. She prayed for the young woman's sake that she did.

The ground lasted a good deal longer than Rebecca had thought it would. There was time to watch the sunrise and listen to more helicopters come and go, but they never came close enough to warrant getting out and trying to signal them.

The day dawned in much the same way the previous one had: gray and gloomy and with a profound sense of loneliness that broke hearts and inspired poets. After a while, it began to rain, but they were all used to that now. It had rained for so long before this whole mess it seemed only fitting that it would end the same way. This was the Pacific Northwest after all and for Rebecca's money, there was no place more beautiful.

The patter of rain soothed her almost as much as the weight of her dog did and she wondered vaguely if it would lull her to sleep.

And then, it did.

19802999R00042

Made in the USA
Middletown, DE
05 May 2015